Here we are again, back in the 1950s! It was the decade that saw a lightening of spirits following a period that had been overshadowed by the Second World War. It also brought us Rock 'n' Roll (which was here to stay) and the hula-hoop (which has been around ever since). It was a decade of change which saw the word "teenager" come into use and a new invader in many homes, as television really took off as a form of entertainment. Changes were also afoot in the lives of "The Broons" and "Oor Wullie", who had been appearing weekly in the pages of "The Sunday Post" since 1936, drawn by the talented Dudley D. Watkins. Throughout the 1950s, Watkins, already a brilliant comic artist, continued to develop as a draughtsman and these developments are obvious as we follow the Broons' and Wullie's adventures over the decade.

So sit back and allow us to take you back over half a century to a classic era of fun and laughter.

Printed and published in Great Britain by D. C. Thomson & Co., Ltd.,
185 Fleet Street, London EC4A 2HS.
© D. C. Thomson & Co., Ltd., 2003.
ISBN 0851168361

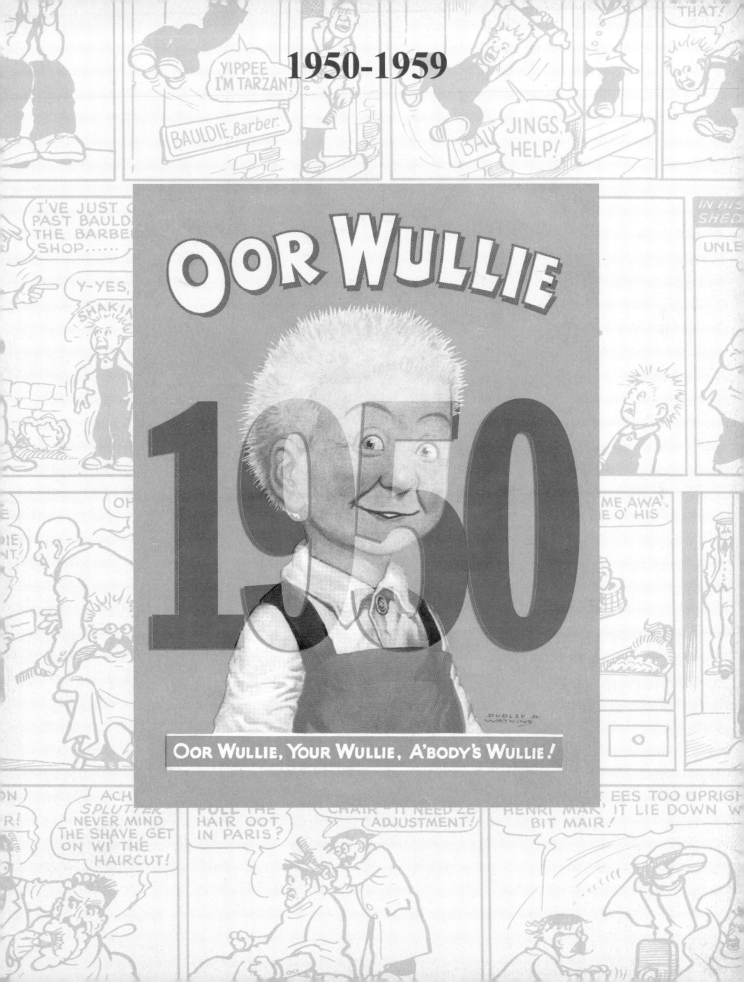

OOR WULLIE 1950-1959

The Sunday Post 29th January 1950

The Sunday Post 8th January 1950

The Sunday Post 12th March 1950

The Sunday Post 12th February 1950

The Sunday Post 28th May 1950

The Sunday Post 26th March 1950

The Sunday Post 2nd July 1950

The Sunday Post 30th April 1950

OOR WULLIE 1950-1959

The Sunday Post 17th September 1950

The Sunday Post 9th July 1950

OOR WULLIE 1950-1959

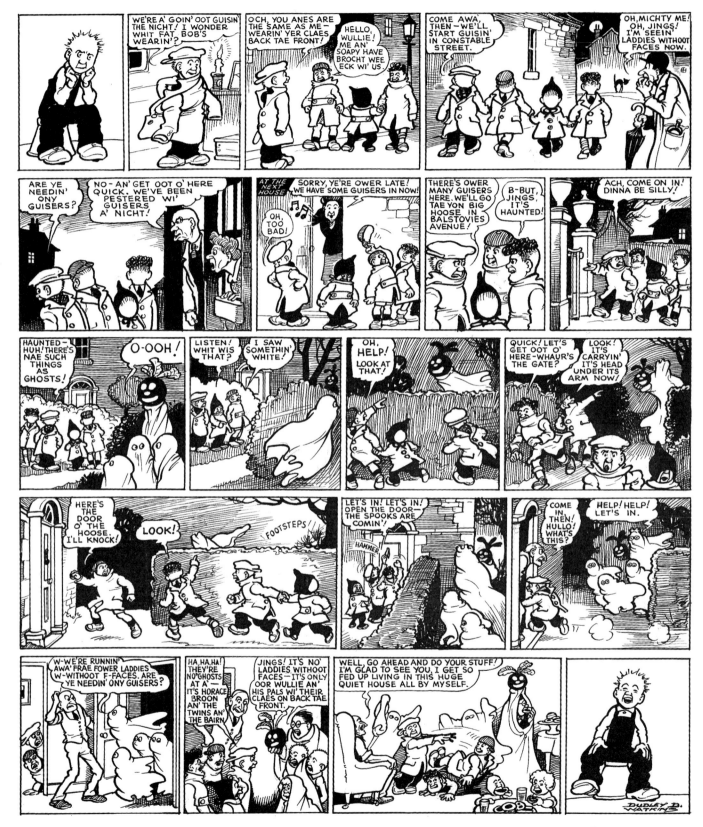

The Sunday Post 29th October 1950

The Sunday Post 12th November 1950

GETTIN' ABOOT!

(Part One)

Oor Wullie's got many ways of getting about, from cartie to bike to skates. The 1950s saw the end of trams as public transport in many Scottish cities, while steam trains were still on track throughout the country and each year saw the latest lines of luxury cars being launched.

●The launch of the Wolseley Four Forty-Four, October 1952.

●Steaming along. The Inverness train leaving Perth Station in March 1953.

●The Vauxhall Victor is launched in 1957.

●Crowds line the streets at Bridge of Dee in May 1958 to watch the journey of Aberdeen's last trams.

●The French Citroen reaches the UK in 1955.

1950-1959

THE BROONS

1951

SCOTLAND'S HAPPY FAMILY THAT MAKES EVERY FAMILY HAPPY!

OOR WULLIE 1950-1959

The Sunday Post 13th May 1951

The Sunday Post 7th January 1951

OOR WULLIE 1950-1959

The Sunday Post 1st July 1951

The Sunday Post 21st January 1951

The Sunday Post 1st April 1951

OOR WULLIE 1950-1959

The Sunday Post 30th September 1951

The Sunday Post 5th August 1951

OOR WULLIE 1950-1959

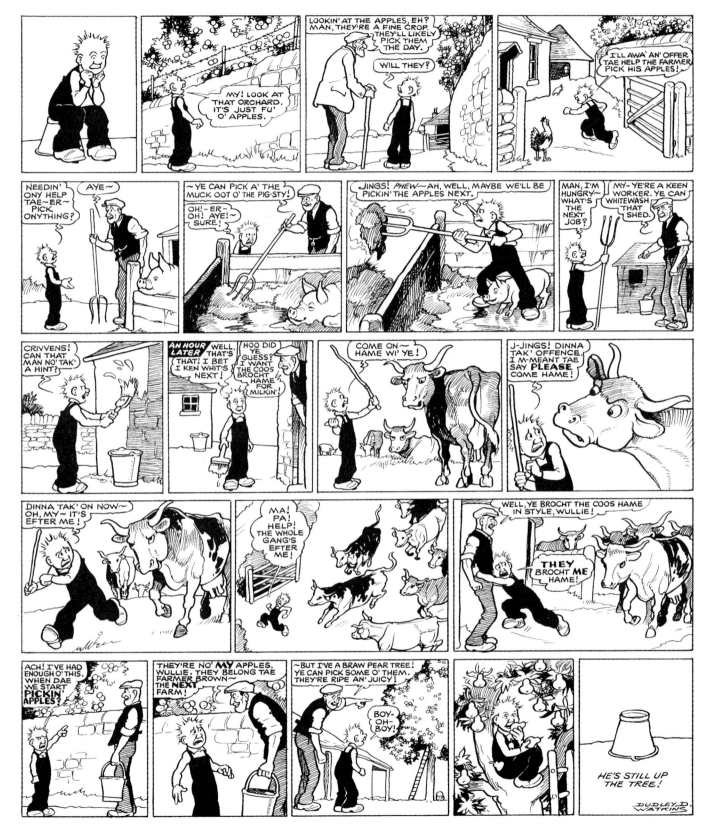

The Sunday Post 14th October 1951

The Sunday Post 19th August 1951

OOR WULLIE 1950-1959

The Sunday Post 14th October 1951

ALL IN FUN

The Broons and Oor Wullie are, of course, famous throughout Scotland and well loved by fans the world over and, to many people, the words "The Sunday Post" conjure up images of Wullie on his bucket and the Broons at home in Glebe Street or holidaying at the But 'n' Ben. What is often forgotten is that The Sunday Post Fun Section in the 1950s was also jam-packed with puzzles, features and cartoon strips. Here are just a few examples from the early part of the decade.

"Nero and Zero, the Rollicking Romans" strip from April 15th, 1952.

"Wonders of the Scottish Counties", part of a regular feature, this particular example is from January 22nd, 1950.

"Nosey Parker" strip from February 5th, 1950.

The Sunday Post 6th January 1952

The Sunday Post 13th January 1952

The Sunday Post 6th April 1952

The Sunday Post 16th March 1952

The Sunday Post 11th May 1952

The Sunday Post 20th April 1952

The Sunday Post 25th May 1952

The Sunday Post 11th May 1952

OOR WULLIE 1950-1959

The Sunday Post 22nd June 1952

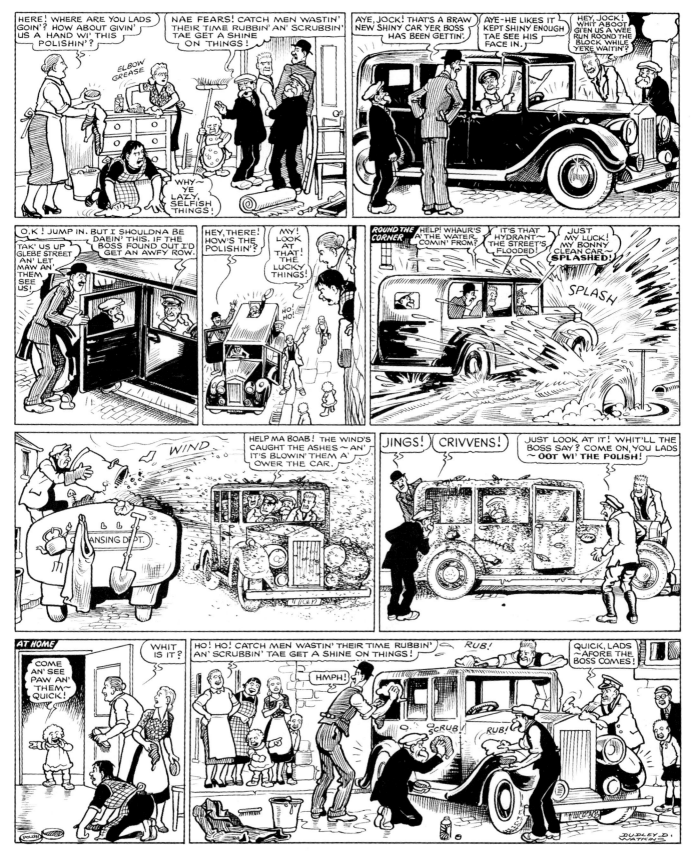

The Sunday Post 18th May 1952

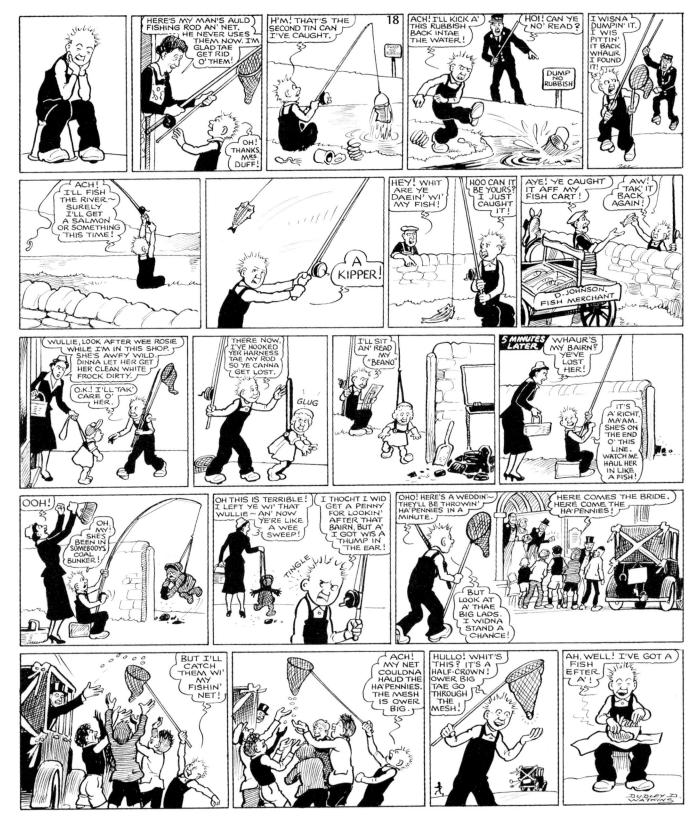

The Sunday Post 27th July 1952

THON'S *Entertainment*

When not sitting at home, chuckling merrily at the antics in the latest Sunday Post Fun Section, just how did we keep ourselves entertained in those far off days before videos and DVDs, satellite, digital and cable television and computer games had entered our homes?

The answer is . . . easily! Most towns had more picture houses than there were pictures to be shown in them, though cinemas soon realised they were under threat from the massive increase in sales of television sets. The television boom started with the rush to buy sets in time for the Coronation, which was transmitted live. The number of homes with a television set in their sitting rooms rose steadily throughout the decade.

Radio remained a popular form of entertainment and, if you wanted to see as well as hear the performers, there was always the theatre or the music hall to visit (though this wasn't always enjoyed so much by the performers, as the legendarily fierce reputation of Glasgow's Empire Theatre among visiting artistes proves).

● Her Majesty's Theatre was typical of local theatres throughout the country.

● Television on tap! A novelty TV design which went on show at the Earls Court Radio Show in 1958.

● Big star names were a regular draw for theatre-goers.

● Just a few of the many cinemas that operated in Dundee in the 1950s.

OOR WULLIE 1950-1959

The Sunday Post 4th January 1953

The Sunday Post 4th January 1953

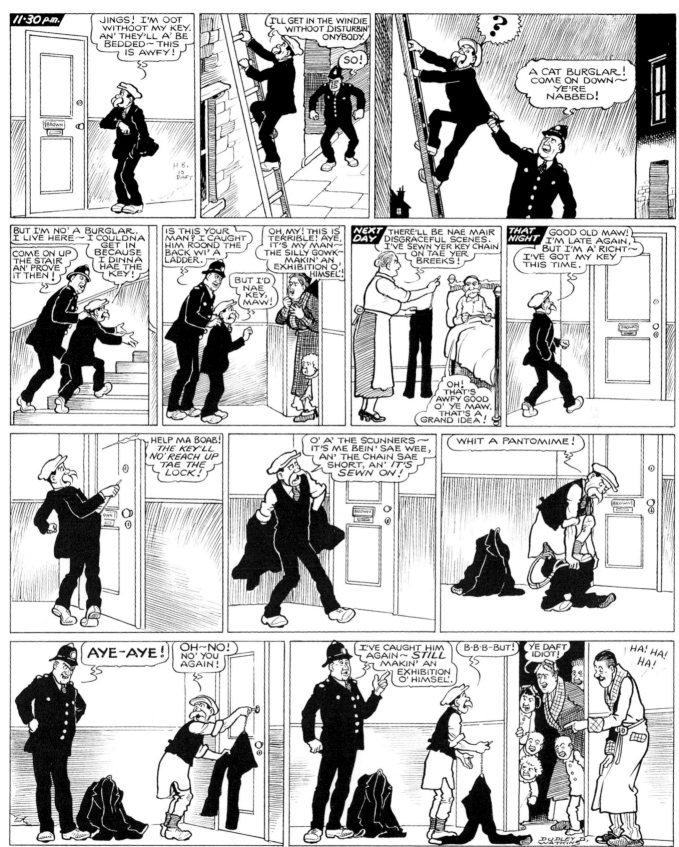

The Sunday Post 15th February 1953

OOR WULLIE 1950-1959

The Sunday Post 3th May 1953

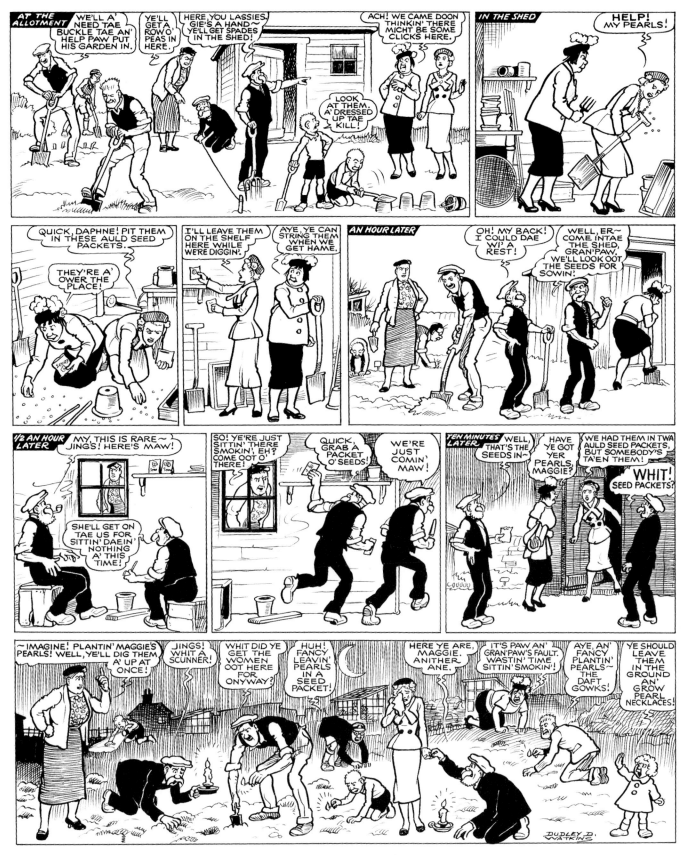

The Sunday Post 5th April 1953

The Sunday Post 9th August 1953

The Sunday Post 20th December 1953

The Sunday Post 16th August 1953

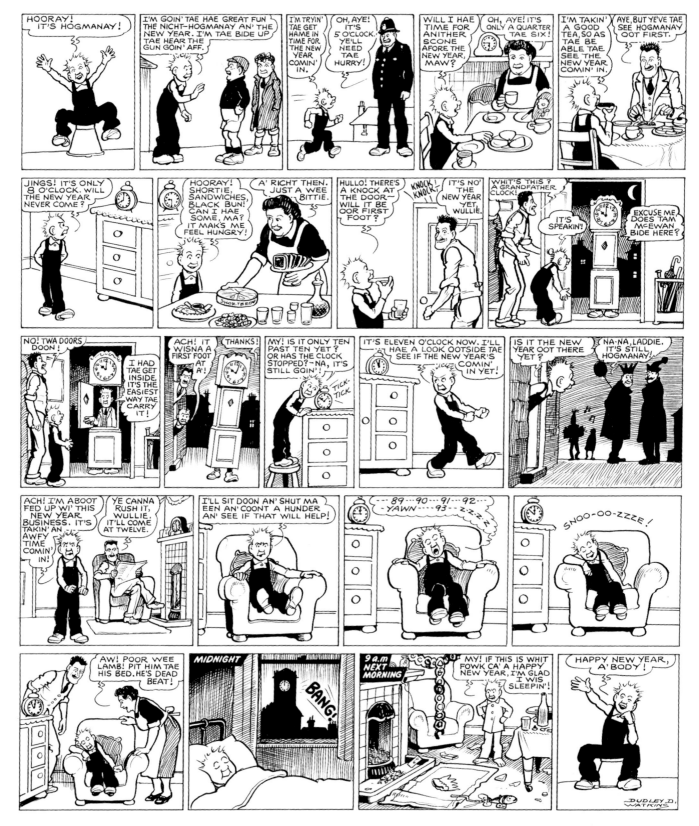

The Sunday Post 27th December 1953

The Sunday Post 18th October 1953

GETTIN' ABOOT!

(Part Two)

●Before the Tay Road Bridge was built, the ferry was the quickest way to get from Dundee to Fife.

●Ships, ahoy! British ships, H.M.S. Broadsword and H.M.S. Crossbow in the harbour. And, sailing from distant shores, the Russian ship Volochaevsk leads the line up.

●Driven round the bend. Buses like this were a familiar sight on the streets of Perth in the late 1950s.

●"When Rangers come to town", is how this photograph was labelled, showing the long line of supporters' buses that arrived in Dundee from Glasgow and across Scotland.

OOR WULLIE 1950-1959

The Sunday Post 10th January 1954

The Sunday Post 3rd January 1954

OOR WULLIE 1950-1959

The Sunday Post 7th March 1954

OOR WULLIE 1950-1959

The Sunday Post 11th April 1954

The Sunday Post 21st March 1954

OOR WULLIE 1950-1959

The Sunday Post 4th July 1954

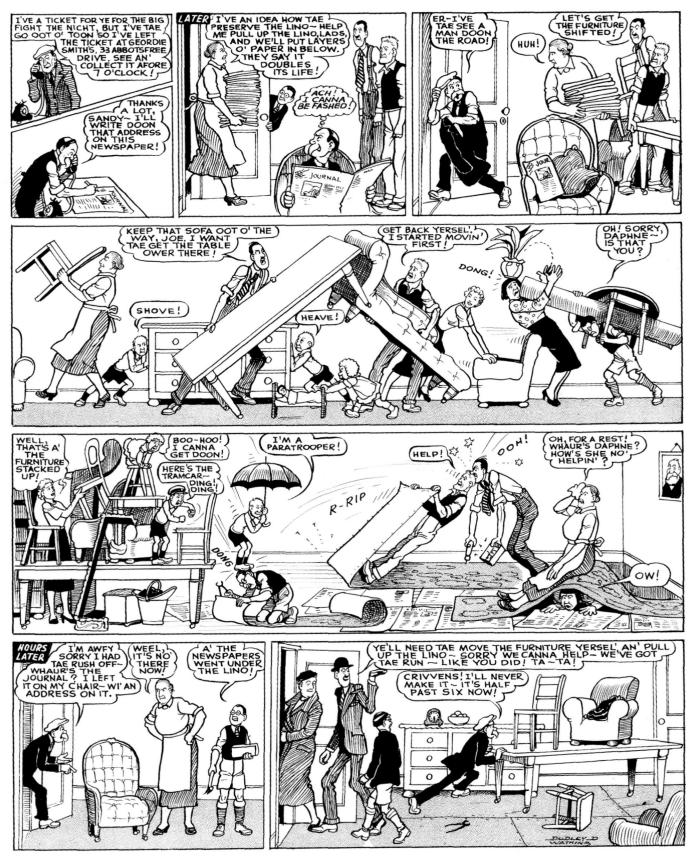

The Sunday Post 9th May 1954

OOR WULLIE 1950-1959

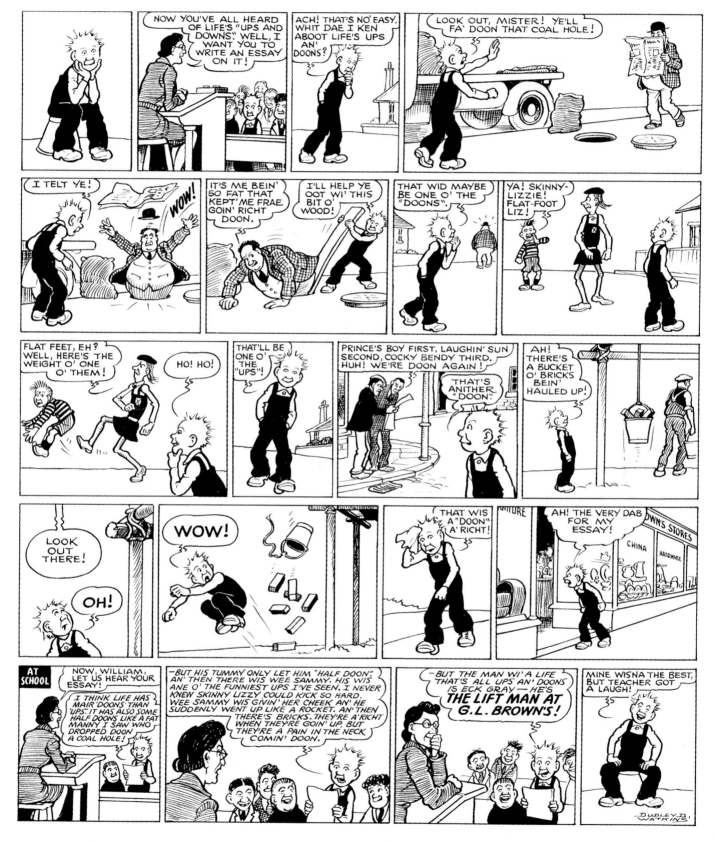

The Sunday Post 17th October 1954

The Sunday Post 16th May 1954

OOR WULLIE 1950-1959

The Sunday Post 28th November 1954

THE BROONS 1950-1959

The Sunday Post 4th July 1954

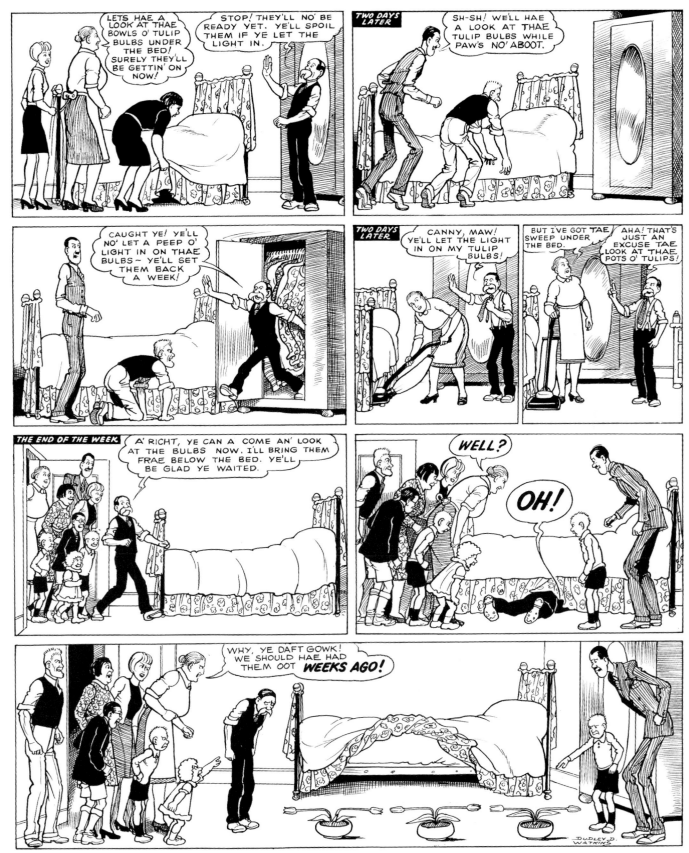

The Sunday Post 24th April 1955

OOR WULLIE 1950-1959

The Sunday Post 27th February 1955

The Sunday Post 15th May 1955

OOR WULLIE 1950-1959

The Sunday Post 27th March 1955

The Sunday Post 5th June 1955

The Sunday Post 29th May 1955

The Sunday Post 24th July 1955

The Sunday Post 12th June 1955

The Sunday Post 4th September 1955

The Sunday Post 3rd July 1955

The Sunday Post 9th October 1955

The Sunday Post 10th July 1955

TOYS AND GAMES

In these days of electronic games and battery operated toys, it's easy to forget that toys were once a lot simpler (but, maybe, a little more fun to play with).

For the laddies, tanks and forts and diggers!

For the lassies, dollies and prams. (And just look at all the toys and games in the background, from Christmas of 1959.)

TOYS

I WONDER WHAT I'LL BUY! I DON'T WANT TO WASTE MY MONEY!

Toys for all ages at the Model Railway Hobby Show.

LATER

TELL ME, SONNY, HOW MUCH DO YOU HAVE TO SPEND?

The Sunday Post 29th January 1956

The Sunday Post 25th March 1956

OOR WULLIE 1950-1959

The Sunday Post 6th May 1956

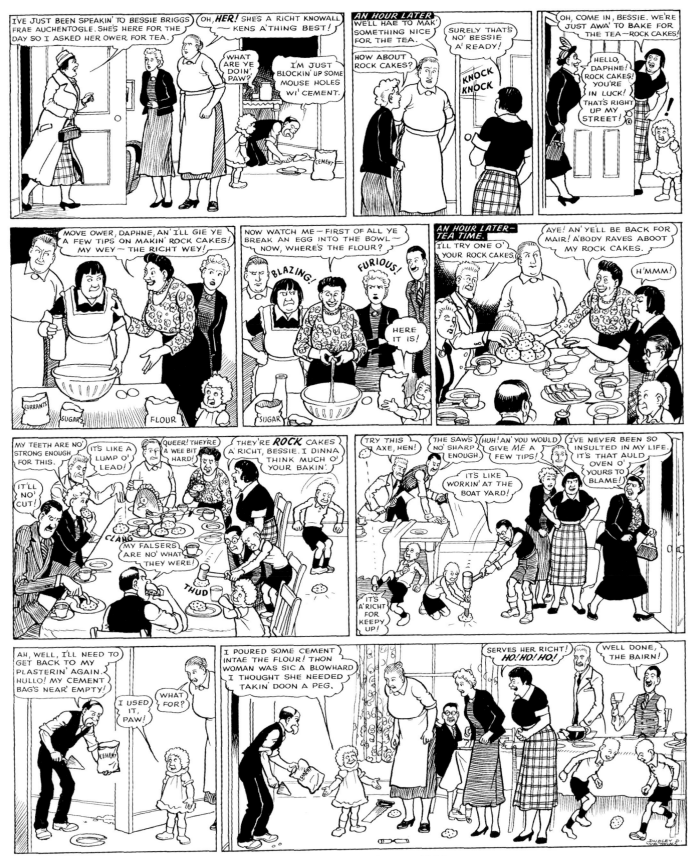

The Sunday Post 13th May 1956

OOR WULLIE 1950-1959

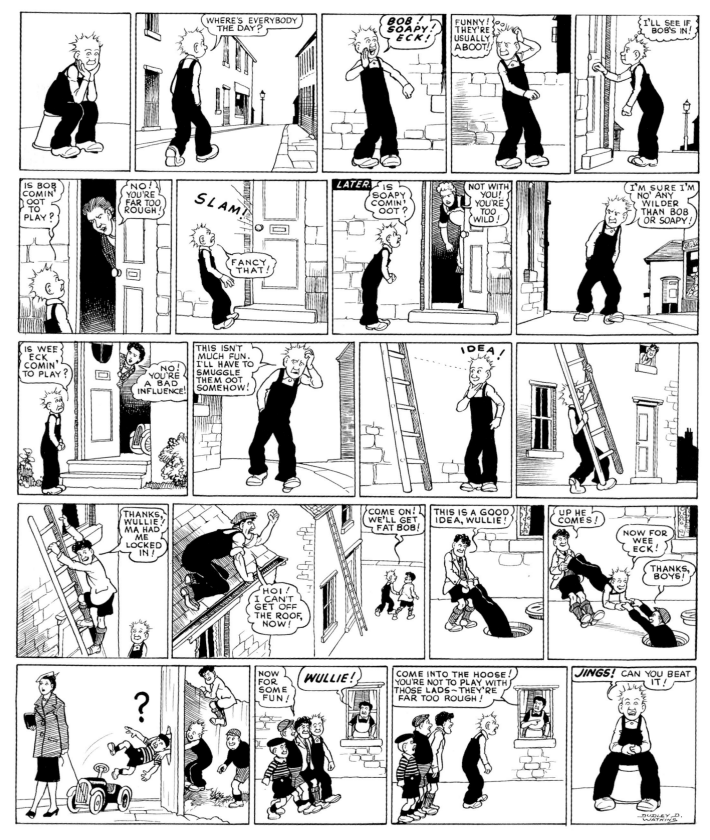

The Sunday Post 20th May 1956

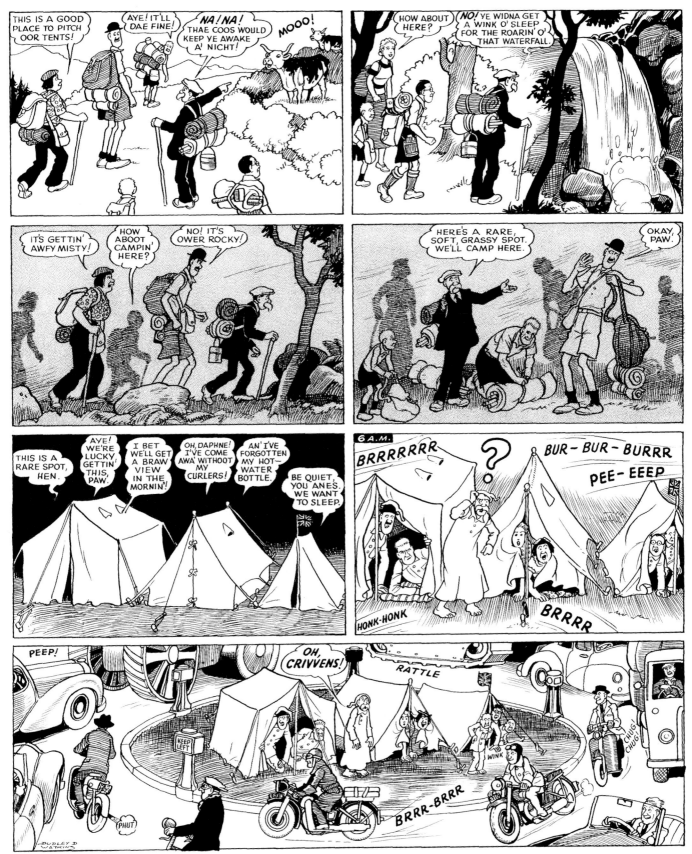

The Sunday Post 1st July 1956

OOR WULLIE 1950-1959

The Sunday Post 28th October 1956

The Sunday Post 23rd September 1956

OOR WULLIE 1950-1959

The Sunday Post 11th November 1956

The Sunday Post 4th November 1956

OOR WULLIE 1950-1959

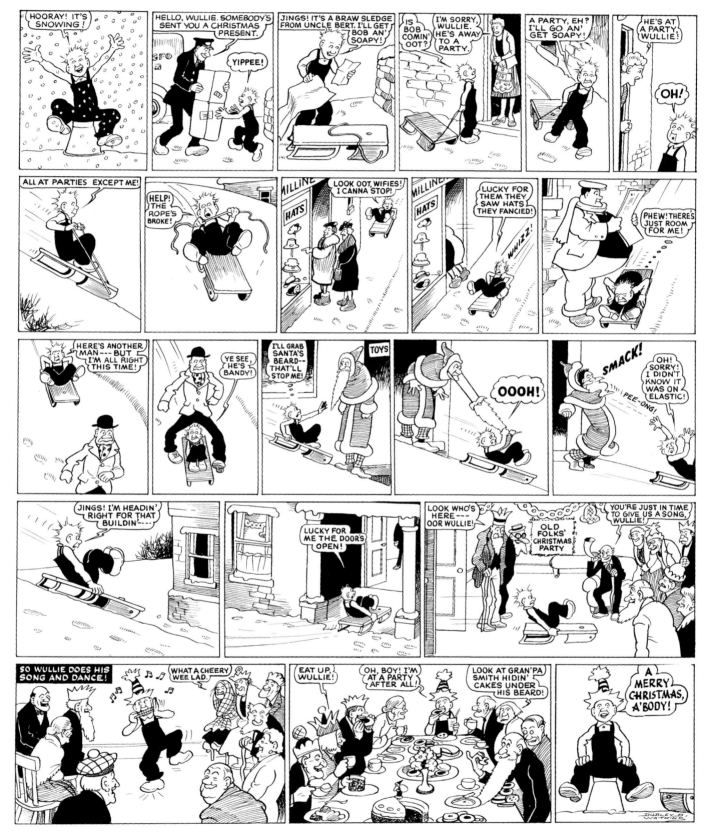

The Sunday Post 23rd December 1956

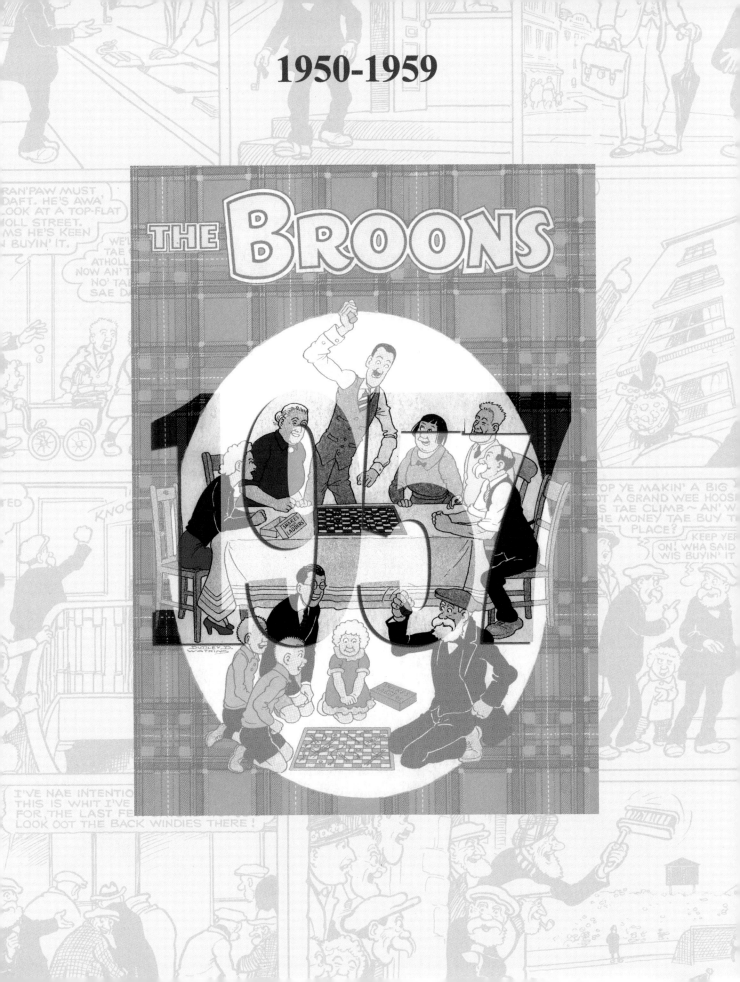

OOR WULLIE 1950-1959

The Sunday Post 17th February 1957

The Sunday Post 10th March 1957

OOR WULLIE 1950-1959

The Sunday Post 14th April 1957

The Sunday Post 14th April 1957

The Sunday Post 21st April 1957

The Sunday Post 28th April 1957

OOR WULLIE 1950-1959

The Sunday Post 7th July 1957

The Sunday Post 11th August 1957

OOR WULLIE 1950-1959

The Sunday Post 15th September 1957

The Sunday Post 10th November 1957

OOR WULLIE 1950-1959

The Sunday Post 22nd September 1957

The Sunday Post 8th December 1957

SCOTLAND THE BRAVE (No. 16)

Scots Sleuth

WHOO-OOO

Allan Pinkerton was born in Glasgow but, in 1840, he emigrated to America, where he founded the Pinkerton Detective Agency, which bears the badge of "The eye that never sleeps."

Pinkerton was a cooper in Dundee, Illinois, but showed such talent as a detective that he changed his job. One of his first murder cases was solved by introducing a tube, which mooned all night, to the murderer's bedroom, forcing him to confess.

The Pinkerton Agency thrived. In 1861, Pinkerton's agents discovered a plot to kill President Abraham Lincoln on his journey from Philadelphia to Washington. Pinkerton himself travelled as bodyguard and men stationed along the route thwarted the plot.

In America's war against crime, the Pinkerton Agency of today still plays a great part. In the last war, Pinkerton agents were engaged in counter-espionage, tracking down spies. Their badge is the reason for private detectives being called "private eyes."

"Scotland The Brave", a feature on heroic Scots which began in 1957. This example is from the 26th of May in that year.

MORE FUN FROM THE FUN SECTION

Here's another look at some of the other features that ran alongside The Broons and Oor Wullie in the Sunday Post throughout the 1950s.

SPOOKY STORIES

McNAB'S VENGEANCE —

Some three hundred years ago there lived on an island in Loch Earn the Neishes, a robber band. As the only boat on the loch was theirs, the Neishes felt secure on their island stronghold. However, after the robbers had attacked a band of his clansmen, McNab of Kinell swore vengeance. To carry out this vow, the McNab clansmen performed a tremendous feat. They dragged a heavy boat

over the mountain range from Loch Tay to Loch Earn. The boat was launched and the avengers rowed stealthily across the loch to the island. Suddenly a piper began to play and the McNabs fell upon the robbers with fire and sword. Only one Neish survived.

This man escaped by swimming the loch but the McNabs, hard on his heels, surrounded him so that his only path lay through a raging torrent. As the McNabs closed in, the surviving Neish leaped into the thundering waters and was never seen again. The McNab chief, too, was killed that night and his ghost is said to appear on the island, while by the river the phantom of the drowned Neish keeps its lonely vigil.

"Spooky Stories", making readers shiver on August 2nd, 1959.

NOSEY PARKER

Nosey almost faints—At what the "artist" paints.

"Nosey Parker" still sticking his nose into everyone's business on August 3rd, 1958.

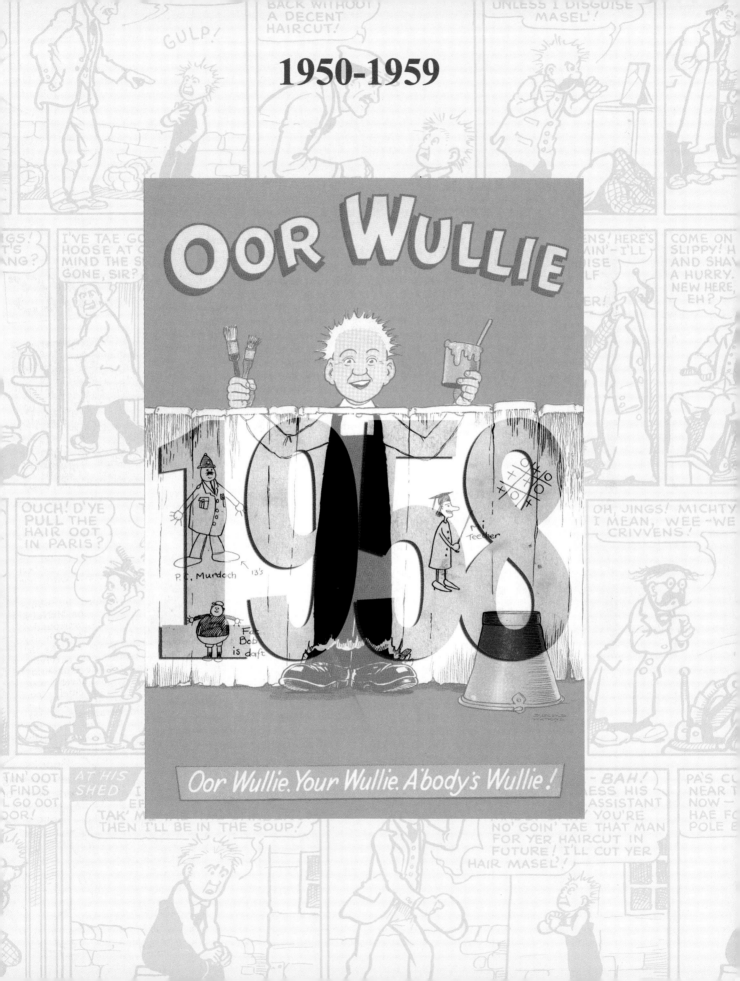

OOR WULLIE 1950-1959

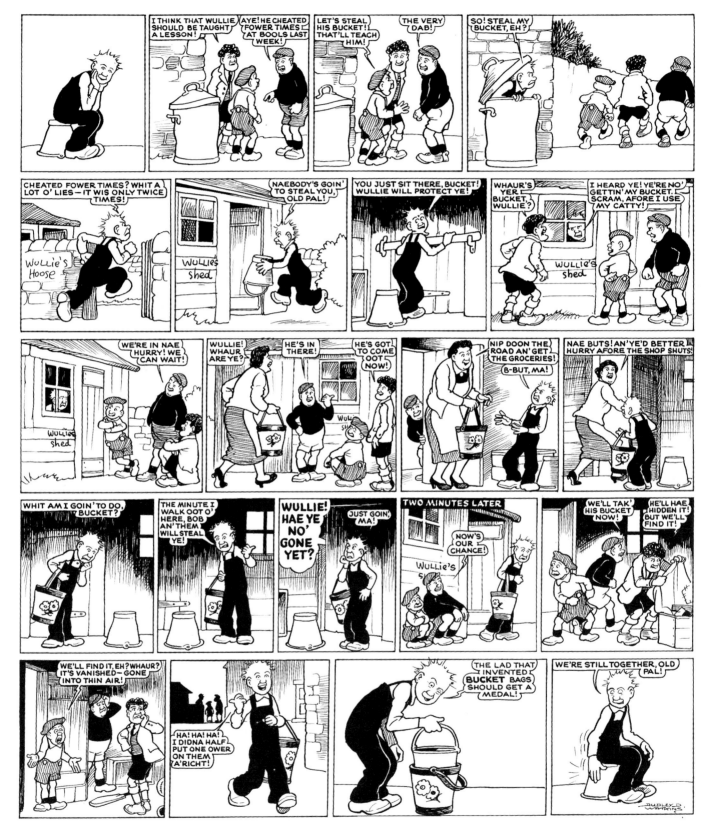

The Sunday Post 2nd February 1958

The Sunday Post 5th January 1958

OOR WULLIE 1950-1959

The Sunday Post 25th May 1958

The Sunday Post 30th March 1958

OOR WULLIE 1950-1959

The Sunday Post 22nd June 1958

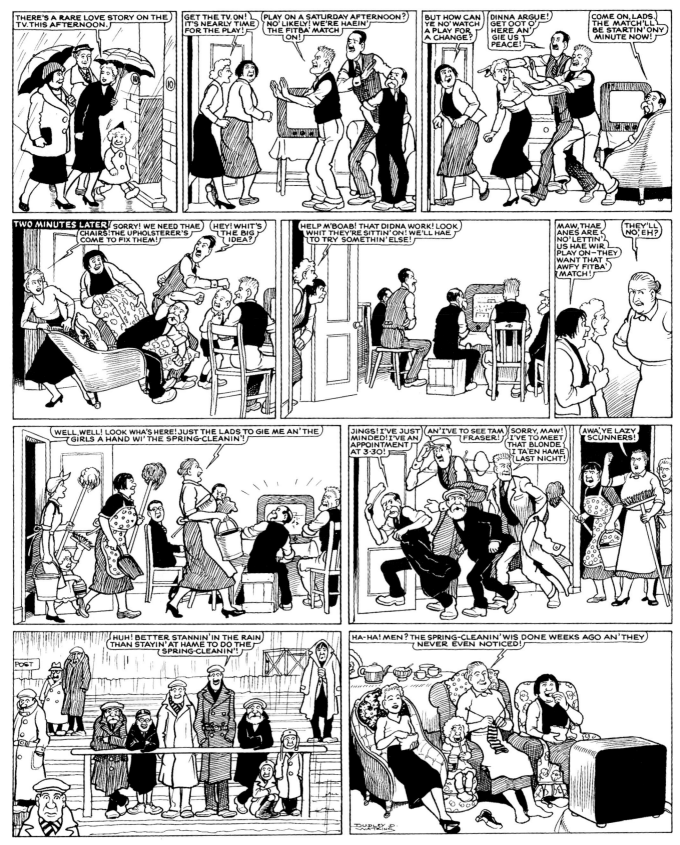

The Sunday Post 27th April 1958

OOR WULLIE 1950-1959

The Sunday Post 29th June 1958

The Sunday Post 22nd June 1958

OOR WULLIE 1950-1959

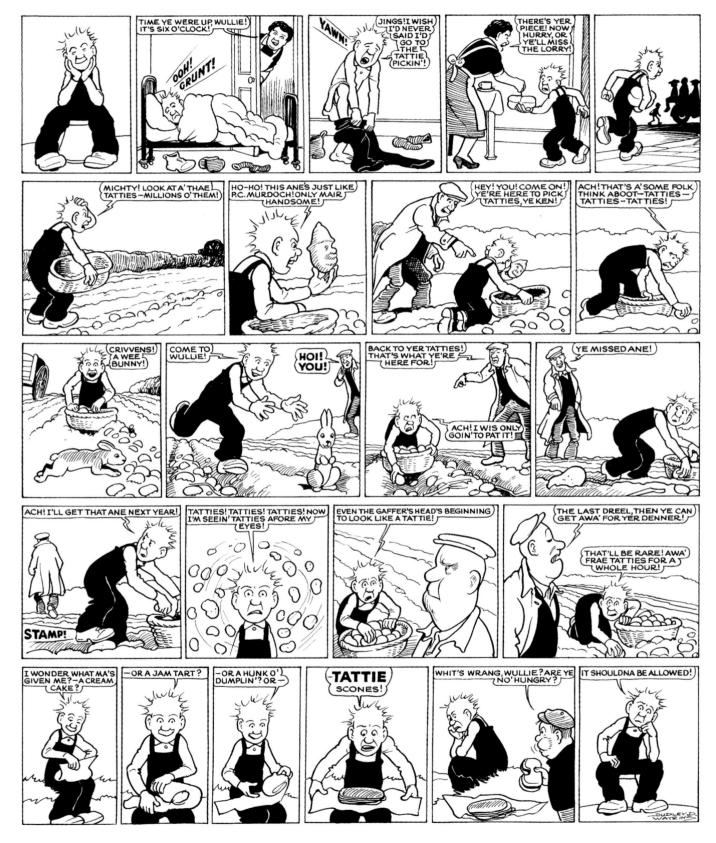

The Sunday Post 28th September 1958

The Sunday Post 26th October 1958

OOR WULLIE 1950-1959

The Sunday Post 23rd November 1958

The Sunday Post 21st December 1958

ON THE BALL

Football was as popular in Scotland of the 1950s as it is now. But, before the dawn of televised matches, the only way to see your team was to be at the game . . . a world away from big screen big match broadcasts.

●1950 League Cup match at Tannadice Park.

●Queue for Cup Final tickets outside Hampden, May 1954.

THIS IS GREAT!

THE TROUBLE IS YE HAVE TO KEEP YER HEAD DOON TO SHINE THE LIGHT ON THE BALL!

●An aerial view of Hampden Park, and a view from the sidelines.

THERE, BOYS! THIS IS BETTER THAN PLAYIN' IN THE STREETS, EH?

JINGS!

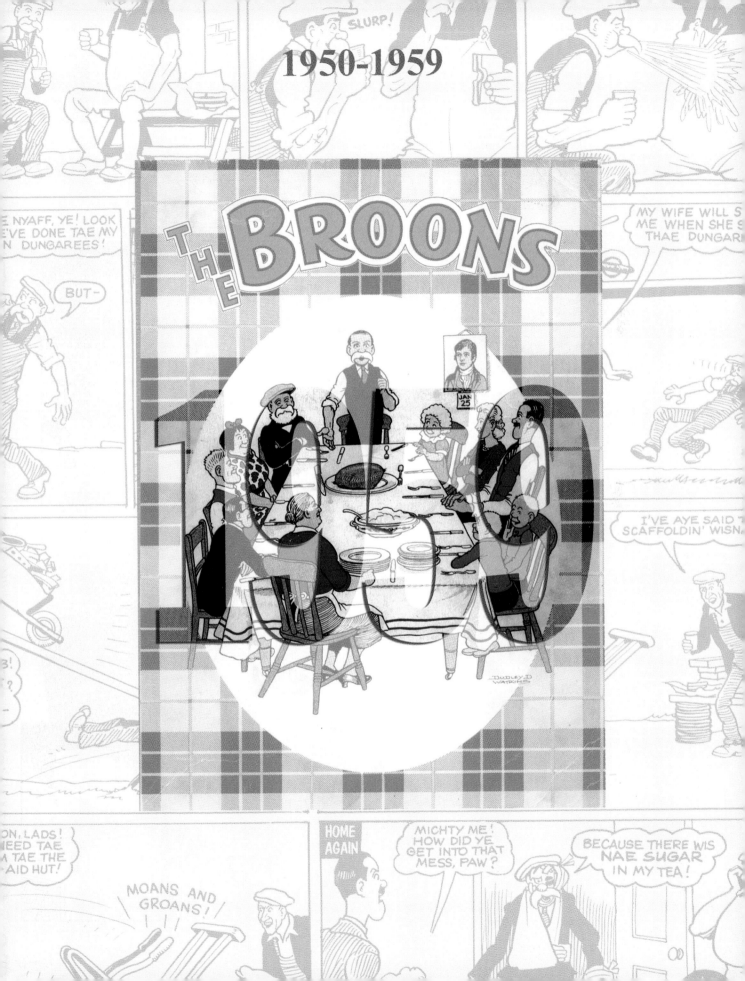

OOR WULLIE 1950-1959

The Sunday Post 3rd May 1959

The Sunday Post 18 January 1959

OOR WULLIE 1950-1959

The Sunday Post 24th May 1959

The Sunday Post 29th March 1959

OOR WULLIE 1950-1959

The Sunday Post 12th July 1959

The Sunday Post 30th August 1959

OOR WULLIE 1950-1959

The Sunday Post 2nd August 1959

The Sunday Post 13th September 1959

OOR WULLIE 1950-1959

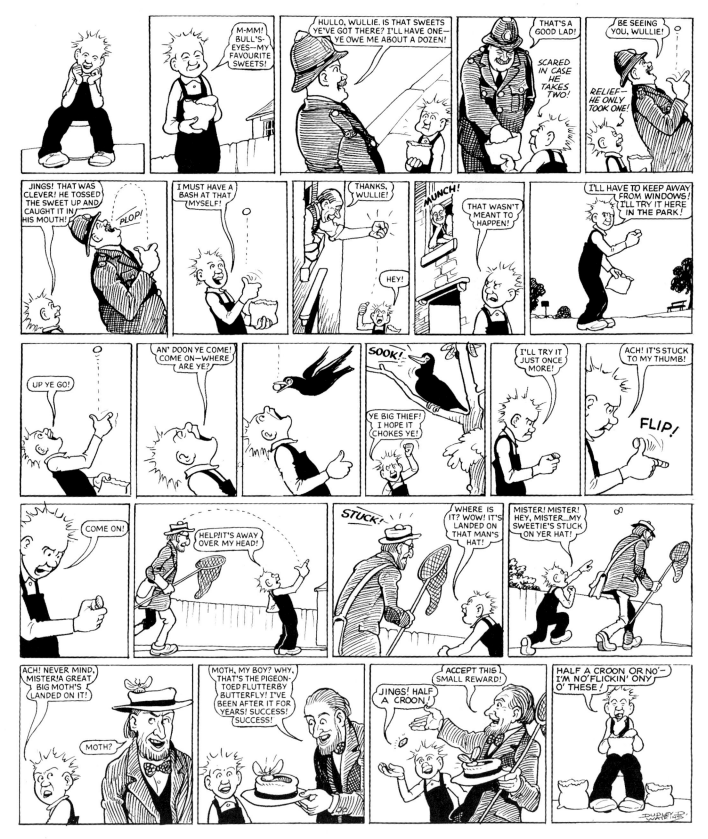

The Sunday Post 23rd August 1959

The Sunday Post 29th November 1959

OOR WULLIE 1950-1959

The Sunday Post 18th October 1959

The Sunday Post 6th December 1959